The Further Adventures of Koko and Moochee

by J.R. Hardin

J. R. Hardin

Published in the United States by BQB Publishing
(Boutique of Quality Books Publishing Company)
www.bqbpublishing.com

Printed in the United States of America

ISBN 978-1-937084-77-6 (p)
ISBN 978-1-937084-78-3 (e)

Library of Congress Control Number: 2012941980

Book design and illustrations by Rob Peters, www.rob-peters.com

Endorsements

"I just finished reading *The Adventures of Little Dog Koko,* and I loved it! In fact, I couldn't put it down. Like the other books J.R. Hardin has written, it has something for everyone: chapter cliffhangers, humor, a touch of mystery, bullying, excitement, friendship, and teamwork. While reading it, I kept thinking, *this is* Home Alone *for dogs!* There's plenty of action and adventure, some very funny scenes, and I love the justice that prevails at the end. Five stars!"

—Susan Magee-Bibi
Youth Services Coordinator for Berks County Public Libraries, Pennsylvania

"Hannah, our oldest daughter, who is ten years old, read *The Adventures of Little Dog Koko* and *The Further Adventures of Koko and Moochee,* and she loved them! She said, 'The Koko books are great. They are exciting and adventurous. Koko is my favorite character because he comes up with great ideas.' She cannot wait for the next one. Our seven-year-old is now going to read them!"

—Jackie Gaskins
Author of *The Four Princesses*

"What a great book! It's action-packed and full of humor. It made me laugh out loud. It would be a super book for adults and children to read aloud together. I can't wait to read about Koko, Moochee, and Tango's next adventure."

– Anne Shoop
Former fourth-grade teacher, interrelated resource teacher for learning disabled and emotionally handicapped children, learner support strategist in Cobb County, Georgia. Former Teacher of the Year at Timber Ridge Elementary School

Also by J.R. Hardin

The Kudzu Monsters

Kalvin the Kudzu Monster

Kudzu Monsters Versus the Creeper Horde

The Adventures of Little Dog Koko

The Kudzu Monster Trilogy

The Perils of Kandi the Kudzu Monster
Coming Spring 2013

Contents

Acknowledgments

I wish to thank my sister, Betty Hertenstein, for editing my books and for the contributions she has made to my stories.

My thanks also go to my publisher, Terri Ann Leidich, for all she has done to promote my books and to Janet Green for her proofreading.

Finally, my appreciation goes to Rob Peters for the excellent job he has done on the book design and for creating my exciting book cover and the inside sketches, and to Katy Whipple for her work with Rob to help bring my book together.

Introduction

Once again, Koko and Moochee are plunged into danger. An old enemy has returned with a gang and seeks revenge on the two little dogs.

The inspiration for this book is my own adopted dog, Koko. The character of Moochee is patterned after my son's adopted dog, Mushu. In this story, I've added a new character—my daughter-in-law's cat, Tango. Tango is a Flame Point Siamese and a bit of a rascal. He is constantly ambushing Koko and Mushu, trying to get them to chase him. But Koko and Mushu are up in years and don't give him a good run. So, the agile feline finds other dogs to chase him. He always loses the dog and then climbs a tree to watch his pursuer search in vain.

This new story is filled with action, suspense, and comedy as Koko and Moochee are pulled into another adventure and find a new friend, Tango.

I hope you enjoy the read.

Chapter One
The Jewel Robbery

Koko heard the doorbell ring and, as usual, was the first one at the door. He loved to greet visitors, but he waited quietly for Mama to open the door.

"Koko, I have a nice surprise for you." Mama winked at the little Shih Tzu as she opened the door. Koko's pal Moochee bounded inside. The two boys happily greeted each other with tails wagging.

Koko had been living with Mama and Dad, his new adopted family, for almost two years. Moochee had been adopted by Mama and Dad's son and his wife. Moochee was spending the week with Koko while Moochee's family was on vacation.

The next morning after Moochee arrived, the two buddies were enjoying an early walk with Mama and Dad. They lived in a quiet neighborhood with few houses around. The little Shih Tzu walked along the side of the road next to Mama, while Dad walked Moochee. It was early summer, and Koko felt frisky in the cool morning air.

Their tranquil walk was interrupted by the faint sound of sirens. Koko caught glimpses of black smoke coming from the town that was over a mile away. *There must be a large fire in town,* he thought.

Just then, a beat-up old van approached them at high speed. As it drew close to them, the van quickly slowed down. A grinning man with a moustache and beard stared at Koko as the van drove past him. Koko looked at him with his one good eye. (His left eye had been blinded in a fight with a German shepherd a couple of years ago.) *That man looks familiar,* thought Koko. *But I can't remember why.*

Later that day, Koko and Moochee rested in the den while Koko's parents watched the local news. A reporter talked about a fire that had destroyed part of a clothing store in town. The police suspected the fire had been set as a diversion while the jewelry store next door was being robbed. Over a hundred valuable rings and necklaces had been stolen. The stolen items were valued at over two hundred and fifty thousand dollars. The police were searching for an escaped convict. They believed he was in the area and may have been involved in the robbery. When the TV showed a picture of the criminal, Koko sat up and stared at the television.

I know that face, he recalled. *That's Stewart, the man who abandoned me in a park years ago and later became a dog thief. But he doesn't look like that picture; he's grown a beard. Stewart was the man driving that van this morning!*

The next day, the dogs were resting in the backyard, which was enclosed by a high wooden fence. Their leisure time was interrupted when a man looked over the fence. The man had a dog treat in his hand.

"Here, pooch," the man called in a pleasant voice, "I have a delicious treat for you."

Moochee wagged his tail and headed toward him.

"Moochee, don't go over there," Koko cautioned him. "You don't know that man, and the treat might have poison in it."

"We used to take food from people all the time when we lived on the street," Moochee responded.

"That was different," Koko told him. "The people knew we were strays. That's why they gave us food. People don't feed other people's dogs in a fenced-in backyard."

Moochee sat down and began to bark at the man. Koko joined in, although he knew Mom and Dad were at church. The man looked around and ran away through the woods behind Koko's house.

"Remember, I saw Stewart drive past us the other day," Koko warned. "We need to be on guard in case he means us harm."

"I'm a lot bigger now," stated Moochee. "If he messes with me, I'll bite him."

"You're not that big," answered Koko. "You're only a little over twice my size, and that's too small to take on a grown human."

Eventually, Koko relaxed and laid his head down. A short time later, their nap was interrupted again by a loud banging noise. They started barking as someone with a heavy hammer knocked two of the boards out of the fence. A face looked through the hole. It was the face of the man who had tried to feed them the treat. He grinned at the barking dogs and disappeared behind the fence.

Moochee started after him.

"Stop, Moochee!" Koko barked. "Remember what I said about being on our guard. Besides, the man has a large hammer."

"No, he doesn't," answered Moochee. "The man leaned the hammer against a tree, and he's running away."

Moochee squeezed through the hole and ran after the man, barking. Koko barked for Moochee to stop chasing the man, but Moochee ignored him and continued the chase. Before he ran after his friend, Koko stuck his head through the hole in the fence and looked around. The man ran to the beat-up old van that Stewart had driven the other day. He retrieved a pole with a looped rope at the end.

That looks like the poles that the dogcatchers use to capture dogs, Koko noted.

Moochee had stopped chasing the man. Now, Koko's friend was weaving between the trees as he ran deep into the woods. The man with the pole was chasing after him.

Koko spun around. He thought he had heard a rustling noise behind him, but he didn't see anything. Then he noticed that the hammer wasn't leaning against the tree.

While Koko stared at the spot where the hammer had been, Stewart stepped out from behind the tree with the hammer in his hand. He raised it above his head and threw it. The little dog saw the heavy object sailing through the air, straight for his head!

Chapter Two
The Chase

Koko rose up on his hind legs and fell backward onto his back. The hammer just missed him and bounced off a tree.

"Benny, chase the dog toward the road," Stewart cried out as he ran toward Koko. "Willard can help you run him down."

Koko jumped to his feet and ran in the direction that Moochee had gone. As he ran close to Benny, the blond, shaggy-headed man took a swipe at him with the pole. Nimbly avoiding the pole, Koko ran to Moochee. The dogs burst out of the woods and onto a paved, two-lane road. Koko heard a motor start and glanced to his right. A very fat man was headed toward them on a motorbike. He had a pole with a looped rope like the one Benny carried.

"I see the dogs!" shouted Willard, the heavyset man. "I'm giving chase on the motorbike."

The motorbike weaved from side to side as Willard tried to drive the bike while balancing the pole on the handlebars. Koko and Moochee ran down the road in front of him.

"He's not a fast driver," Moochee commented as the two dogs began to pull away from Willard.

"That motorbike is too light for someone like him," Koko observed. "He must weigh three hundred pounds."

Koko slowed down but continued to stay a few hundred feet ahead of Willard.

"We need to get off this road," barked Koko. "Stewart and Benny will be after us in the van before long."

"There's a dirt road up ahead on the right," Moochee observed.

"Okay, we'll go down the dirt road; that'll slow Willard some more," Koko agreed. "When we see the van on the dirt road, we'll turn back into the woods."

Behind them, Willard was having a difficult time on the dirt. He kept wobbling back and forth and wasn't traveling much over ten miles an hour. A minute later, Benny drove the van onto the dirt road. He quickly caught up with Willard, but the big man didn't pull to the side and let the van pass him.

"Get out of the way!" Benny yelled and honked the horn.

"Give me time to get off the road!" Willard hollered back. "There's a ditch on each side of me."

While the men were arguing, Koko and Moochee left the road and ran for a wooded thicket. The van pulled off the road. Benny stepped out with his pole and trotted across the grass toward the thicket. The dogs ran between the small trees and into a clump of tall brush. As Willard's motorbike lumbered into the thicket, the little dogs hid under a bush. The ends of the pole that Willard carried across the handlebars caught on a couple of trees. There was a loud crack as the pole broke, and the heavy man was jerked off the seat. He hit the ground hard and lay on his back, moaning. The broken pole was across his chest. The motorbike continued forward for several more yards before it crashed into a tree.

Benny was searching the woods to the left of the dogs when Koko heard something coming through the woods behind them. Koko and Moochee got to their feet and headed to their right, away from the sound. The dogs ran through the thicket until they came to a newly plowed field. About two hundred feet to their right was the dirt road. To their left was a wooded area. As he turned to look behind him, Koko saw that Benny had spotted them.

Benny ran toward the van while Willard staggered toward his motorbike and tried to start it. The dogs trotted into the field as Benny drove slowly along the road, keeping pace with Koko and Moochee.

I wonder what Stewart is doing, thought Koko. *I'm sure he's somewhere around here. The sound coming from the woods behind us might be him.*

"Let's head for that farmhouse and barn up ahead," suggested Moochee. "Maybe the people there will help us."

About that time, Willard came out of the thicket on the motorbike. Koko turned to see Willard slipping and sliding across the muddy field toward them. The dogs turned toward the farm and discovered that Benny had left the van. The shaggy-headed crook was between them and the farmhouse. Moochee turned to his right and ran toward the patch of woods. As he turned to race after him, Koko saw Moochee put on the brakes.

"What's wrong?" barked Koko.

"Something big is moving in the woods," Moochee whispered.

All of a sudden, Stewart burst out of the woods with a pole, ran past Moochee, and charged toward Koko. He thrust the pole at Koko, but the little dog dodged to his right and ran toward Willard. The fat man tried to head off Koko, but the motorbike slid out from under him. Willard landed facedown in the mud. As Koko ran past him, he stepped on Willard's head. Stewart slapped at the little dog with the pole, missed, and struck Willard on the back.

As he tried to get away, Moochee slipped and fell in the mud. Climbing to his feet, Moochee ran to his right. Benny was a few feet in front of him, trying to make the loop on his pole bigger. The pole flew from Benny's hands when Moochee crashed into him. Both of them toppled into the muddy field. Benny reached out and grabbed Moochee around the middle. But the muddy dog squirted through his fingers like a greased pig. As Benny leaned to his side to retrieve his pole, Moochee ran past him. Standing in front of Moochee was Willard, wiping mud from his face. Coming

toward the trapped dog from behind was Benny. Willard's legs were spread apart to help him keep his balance in the mud. Moochee ran between Willard's legs. The big man grabbed the muddy dog but couldn't hold on to him. Willard lost his balance and fell forward. As he went face forward into the muddy field again, his head hit Benny in the stomach.

Koko ran past the two crooks to Moochee, and the dogs raced toward the farmhouse. Willard and Benny were just getting to their feet again when Stewart tried to run around them. Benny whirled around and accidentally hit Stewart in the face with his pole. Stewart fell backward, cracking Willard across his kneecap with his pole. Willard stumbled forward and fell on top of Benny, pushing him down in the mud.

Koko and Moochee slowed down to a trot. As they approached the farm, two large hound dogs charged out of the barn.

"You little dogs made a big mistake walking on our property," one of the big dogs growled. "Me and Butcher Boy are going to chew you to ribbons!"

Koko and Moochee turned to the right and ran for a large wooded area as the big dogs gained on them.

Chapter Three
Tango

Running as fast as they could, Koko and Moochee made it to the woods ahead of the hounds. As Koko raced past a large oak, he caught a glimpse of something white sitting on a branch. Moochee saw it too.

"Koko, did you see that cat up in the tree?" Moochee asked.

"I saw something," answered Koko. "But I couldn't stop to check it out."

Koko heard the big dogs crashing through the brush. Then the sound stopped, followed by a hissing sound and the snarls of the hounds. The big dogs had stopped chasing the little dogs and were barking at the cat. *Boy, it sure is lucky that that cat was in the tree,* Koko sighed just before he bumped into Moochee. Moochee had come to a sudden stop.

"What's wrong?" Koko asked.

"There's a ditch in front of me," Moochee whined, "and there's water flowing at the bottom."

Koko looked in the ditch. "The ditch isn't very deep," Koko observed, "and the water is very shallow. It won't hurt us to jump in the ditch and follow the stream. We can't stay here; the big dogs may come after us again."

"Okay," Moochee reluctantly agreed. "But I don't like jumping into water. It might get deeper and wash us over a waterfall."

The dogs jumped in the ditch and waded through the water. Their stomachs just touched the water as they splashed along. The baying of the hounds got further away, until they could barely hear it. The sides of the ditch became higher, and there was a drop-off ahead of them.

"See, I told you," Moochee whined. "There's a waterfall ahead."

When they came to the drop-off, they could see that it was less than a foot high, but there was a small pool of water at the bottom. Koko jumped into the water and discovered it was as deep as it looked. His feet barely touched the ground. Koko held his head up to keep it dry, but a wave splashed over him when Moochee jumped in.

"You dogs are funnier than a box full of chipmunks," said a voice above them.

Koko looked up and saw a white cat with pale eyes looking down at them.

"We're not splashing through this water for your amusement," Moochee growled. "We're trying to lose some big dogs that are chasing us."

"Don't worry about those hounds," answered the cat. "They're still barking up a tree that I left five minutes ago."

"How did you leave without them spotting you?" Koko asked.

"I have a way of sneaking from one tree to another," answered the feline as he licked his paws.

"What did you mean when you said we were funnier than a box of chipmunks?" Moochee barked.

"I was watching those men chase you around that field," the cat replied. "I laughed so hard that I fell out of the tree."

"It wasn't funny to us!" Moochee barked even louder. "Those men were trying to hurt us!"

"Don't bark so loud, Moochee," Koko cautioned. "The hounds have stopped baying; they may have heard you."

"Don't worry about them," the cat confided. "They don't wander very far from the farm. Besides, you should thank me for stopping those hounds before they caught you."

"Yes, I heard you hiss at them," answered Koko. "Did you do that to get their attention?"

"Of course," purred the cat. "You're too much fun. I couldn't let you get mauled by those dumb hounds."

Koko thanked the cat, but Moochee just snorted and turned his head away.

"My name is Koko, and my buddy is Moochee. What's your name?"

"People call me Tango. I'm a Siamese."

"Siamese cats have darker faces than you do," argued Moochee.

"I'm a special breed of Siamese," Tango stated. "I've heard that I'm orange and white rather than chocolate and white."

"Whatever," Moochee conceded.

"Come on, Moochee," urged Koko. "We need to get out of this stream."

The dogs waded through the stream until they came to a high bank with a road at the top. Tango walked above them, twitching his tail and purring. Koko and Moochee started to climb the bank, then stopped when they spotted the white van headed their way. The stream passed through a large drainpipe, which ran under the road. The dogs ran down the bank and into the drain. The van stopped on the road above them. Koko and Moochee listened for doors opening, but the men remained in the van.

"Those mutts must be somewhere in this area," snarled Stewart.

"Why do you want those dogs?" asked Benny. "We should be getting out of this state before the police catch us."

"We can't leave just yet," Stewart replied. "The police are looking for me. I need to lay low at Willard's fishing cabin for another week or so."

"We should be at the cabin and not out in the open looking for those dogs," Willard fussed.

"I want those dogs," shouted Stewart, "especially the little black one! They were the reason I ended up in prison. When I get my hands on them, I'm going to kill them."

Moochee let out a deep growl when he heard what Stewart said.

"Did you hear that growl?" Benny cried. "There's a wild animal out there!"

"It might be a dog out there," answered Stewart.

Another growl came from a tree. Tango sat on a limb above the men, growling. "There's your wild beast," laughed Willard. "A stupid cat is growling at us."

Tango didn't like that last remark and hissed at the men.

"Get out of here, cat!" shouted Stewart.

Tango jumped out of the tree and ran into the drain.

"Let's go back to my cabin," Willard pleaded. "I'm getting hungry."

"Okay," Stewart snapped. "We'll go back to that shack you call a cabin so you can stuff your fat face."

The van drove away and the dogs relaxed.

"Thanks for growling," Koko told Tango.

"That's okay," Tango replied. "I'm enjoying all the action that you guys attract. Besides, I don't like those men."

The dogs left the drain and started looking for home, but nothing looked familiar to them. They were completely lost. They came to a neighborhood, but the other dogs weren't friendly to them. A big Doberman pinscher growled and started after Moochee, but he put on the brakes when Tango ran past him in the opposite direction. The cat was a very fast runner, but so was the Doberman. The big dog was getting closer to Tango every second. In the nick of time, the Siamese ran under a raised deck at the back of a house, dove through a wooden lattice, and raced toward a large oak tree. The Doberman couldn't get through the lattice and had to turn around to get out from under the deck. By that time, Koko and Moochee had disappeared into a wooded area, and Tango was resting in a tree. The big dog searched and sniffed the air but couldn't find the crafty feline.

The threesome left the neighborhood and journeyed deeper into the woods. Koko and Moochee went to bed hungry that night, but Tango caught a field mouse for his dinner. He offered to catch some mice for the dogs, but they declined his offer.

Chapter Four
The Hideout

In the morning, the trio followed the paved road but kept in the woods when possible. Whenever they came across a side road, they ventured down it to see if it looked familiar or led to somewhere they could find food. If a vehicle approached, they quickly hid and waited for it to pass.

The dogs had just come to a dirt road when they heard the whining sound of a small motor. As they hid in some brush, they saw Willard on the motorbike. He turned onto the dirt road and disappeared down a hill.

"Let's stay in the woods and follow the road. Maybe we can find out where Willard went," Koko suggested.

"Why not just go the other way," Moochee argued. "We'll just find more trouble following him."

"I say follow the fat man," Tango added. "It's bound to lead to more adventure."

"If we know where Stewart and his gang are hiding," Koko replied, "we might find out what they're planning."

"I don't care what they're planning," Moochee stated.

"If we can find out their plans, it could keep us from getting caught," Koko added. "Besides, we might be able to recover the stolen jewels and send Stewart back to prison."

"You're probably right," whined Moochee. "But we'll be putting ourselves in danger again."

"Oh boy," Tango exclaimed, "more adventure and excitement!"

"That cat's not right in the head," Moochee stated.

They crept through the woods and followed the dirt road to a rustic wooden shack. Willard's motorbike and Stewart's van were parked in front of the cabin. The fishing cabin was sitting on brick foundation columns. The front was half a foot off the ground, but the back was a foot and a half higher. This was because the shack was built on the side of a hill that sloped down to a small lake. The cabin had a front door with two windows on the front and two on the back of the house.

"Moochee and Tango," whispered Koko. "Stay hidden while I check out the fishing cabin."

Koko crept through the woods until he was at the side of the cabin where there were no windows. As he left the safety of the trees, his heart pounded in his small chest. He darted out of the bushes and ran under the shack. He could hear Stewart's voice coming from inside the shack.

Koko could see into the room through several small cracks between the floorboards. Stewart opened a small canvas bag and took a diamond necklace out of it.

"This necklace is worth about forty thousand dollars just by itself," Stewart declared. "I'd estimate the jewels we got from the robbery are valued between two hundred and fifty to three hundred thousand dollars. I have a fence that'll buy them for half that amount, so I'll have no problem paying each of you twenty-five thousand dollars."

Benny looked happy, but Willard was frowning. Koko jumped as Tango rubbed up against him. Moochee was also under the shack, peeking through a crack and licking his lips. Creeping from under the cabin, Koko motioned the others to follow.

"I thought you were still in the woods," Koko scolded. "I nearly bumped my head on the floor when Tango rubbed against me."

"Well, Tango followed you under the cabin, and I didn't want to stay in the woods by myself," Moochee replied.

"The stolen jewels are in that small canvas bag," Koko related. "Maybe we can figure a way to get that bag."

"Well, I noticed Willard kept getting sandwiches out of a picnic basket," Moochee added. "I think we should swipe the food first."

"If you wanted food, why didn't you take the dead mouse I offered you?" Tango questioned.

"Can I bite him just once?" Moochee barked.

"Tango is our friend," answered Koko. "He's lured big dogs away from us on two occasions."

"You can't bite me, chubby dog," stated Tango, "because you aren't fast enough to catch me. I'm going to catch my lunch while you think about getting food away from Willard. I don't think that will be as easy as catching a mouse."

Tango leapt over a bush and slipped into the woods.

"I agree with you," Koko told Moochee. "We do need food. I have a plan, but it'll be risky. We'll wait for Tango to return before we try it."

A couple of hours later, Moochee hid in the woods where he could see the front door. Koko watched Tango climb a tree, then jump onto the roof of the shack. Up there, the cat would get a good view of the action. Koko sat down in front of the cabin and began to bark. The front door swung open, and Koko ran down the hill toward the lake.

"It's that little, black dog!" yelled Willard.

Stewart and Benny shoved past him and ran after the little dog with their dogcatcher poles. Koko paced back and forth in front of the lake as if he didn't know which way to go. When Stewart and Benny got closer, he ran into the woods. The two robbers ran into the woods after him. Willard didn't follow Koko like the little dog hoped he would. The big man just stood at the top of the hill and watched.

Just then, Tango jumped off the roof, landed on Willard's head, leapt to the ground, and darted under the van. The thief screamed and chased after Tango. Koko glanced over to see Willard on his hands and knees, trying to grab Tango. Emerging from the woods unnoticed, Moochee slipped into the cabin while Willard was occupied with Tango. Once Koko saw Moochee trot out of the shack with the handle of the picnic basket between his teeth, he barked and ran deeper into the woods. Before he ran into the thick brush, the little dog turned to see Tango disappear into the woods.

A short time later, Koko joined Tango and Moochee at the top of a hill where they could look down on the lake and cabin. The crooks were still searching the woods below them. As Koko tore the wrapper off a cheese sandwich, he noticed that Moochee had already eaten a couple of sandwiches. Some of the sandwiches were cheese, some were peanut butter, and some were egg with olive slices. Koko and Tango nibbled at the food, but Moochee gobbled it down so fast that he got a stomachache.

Chapter Five
A Dangerous Mission

It was late in the day when Koko, Moochee, and Tango snuck down to the shack. They watched from the bushes as Stewart come up from the lake and entered the fishing cabin. Koko and Moochee quickly ran to the cabin and listened under the floor. Tango followed them at a slow pace. Benny and Willard were inside, arguing about the missing sandwiches.

"I think you ate all the food and hid the basket in the woods," snapped Benny, pointing his finger at Willard.

"There were ten sandwiches in the basket," Willard stated. "You and Stewart each had one, and I had three. That left five sandwiches. My stomach isn't big enough to hold eight sandwiches."

"Your stomach is big enough to hold twenty sandwiches!" Benny shouted back.

"The chubby dog may have stolen our sandwiches," Stewart added. "I saw his paw prints on the step by the front door. He could have come in and grabbed the basket while we were chasing the little dog and the cat."

"That's pretty clever," Benny whispered.

"Dogs aren't that smart," declared Willard.

"Don't underestimate those dogs," warned Stewart. "I ended up in jail because of them."

Under the floor, Tango twitched his tail and Koko sniffed the air.

"Something stinks down here," whispered Tango.

"Yes, I smell something, too," Koko confirmed.

"Sorry about that," Moochee whispered. "Those egg sandwiches are giving me gas."

The gas fumes drifted up into the cabin. Benny began sniffing the air.

"Who cut the cheese?" Benny asked as he stared at Willard.

"Don't look at me," insisted Willard.

"Willard, go stand outside!" shouted Stewart.

"It's not me," whined Willard as he went out the door.

Koko watched as Willard walked up the dirt road, still complaining that he didn't do anything. The dogs and cat retreated to the bushes to talk over Koko's plan for retrieving the stolen jewels.

"We'll do the same thing we did before," Koko told them. "I'll bark and get them to chase me. When all the crooks are chasing me, Moochee can run into the cabin, grab the bag of jewels, and run into the woods. If you need some help, Moochee, Tango will back you up."

"It sounds too risky to me," Tango commented. "And risks don't normally bother me."

"Moochee won't go into the cabin if any of the thieves are close by," added Koko. "Tango, you keep watch on the roof and warn Moochee if one of the men heads back to the cabin."

Again, Koko ran to the cabin door and barked. As soon as the door started to open, he ran toward the woods. It was a good thing that Koko didn't wait, because Stewart ran out with the pole and nearly got him. Koko raced into the woods with all three men chasing him. Stewart followed the same path Koko took, while the other two men went to either side of him. Tango climbed on top of the roof as Moochee ran into the shack.

Koko weaved through the woods, glancing toward the cabin from time to time. When Moochee didn't come out the door, Tango jumped to a tree and through a window into the cabin.

Benny and Stewart saw the cat, stopped chasing Koko, and hurried toward the cabin. Koko barked out a warning, and Tango jumped out the window to the tree. As Benny tried to enter the cabin, Moochee bolted out the door.

Moochee ran past Benny, but the crook dove forward and grabbed Moochee's hind leg. Moochee spun around and bit Benny's hand, and the crook released his leg. But before Moochee could get away, Stewart looped a rope around his neck. Moochee was caught!

Koko circled through the woods and ran under the cabin floor. A few minutes later, Willard ran out of the woods with his hands formed into fists.

"That's the dog that stole our sandwiches!" Willard shouted as he ran toward Moochee. "I'll punch and stomp on him until he's as flat as a rug."

"I have a better idea." Stewart stopped him. "Get the rope out of the van and tie him to that tree. We'll use him to lure the little black dog to us."

The crooks tied Moochee to the tree and went into the cabin to watch. Every time Moochee tried to bite the rope, Benny ran out of the cabin and kicked him. Moochee quit biting the rope and lay on the ground as night approached.

Koko entered the woods and found Tango.

"Why did you enter the cabin?" Koko asked.

"Moochee barked that he couldn't reach the bag on the table," Tango explained. "I was shoving on the bag when we heard your warning."

"Okay, I have a plan for freeing Moochee," Koko replied. "I'll tell it to you while we wait for it to get dark."

"It had better be a good plan," Tango insisted. "The bad men will be expecting you to try to rescue Moochee."

Chapter Six
Prisoner Swap

As the day drew dark, Koko hid behind a bush not far from Moochee. Tango walked up to Moochee to tell him the plan.

"Hi, Moochee," Tango meowed. "It looks like Koko was right. He said the crooks tied you up to lure him in and they wouldn't try to capture me as long as I didn't try to free you. In a moment, Koko is going to run up to you and gnaw on the rope."

"Tell him not to do it!" Moochee exclaimed. "I'm being watched. If Koko tries to free me, he'll get captured."

"As soon as the bad men come out of the shack," Tango explained, "he'll take off running and try to get them to chase him. While they're chasing Koko, you can chew through the rope."

At that moment, Koko burst from the woods, ran to Moochee, and started to chew the rope. An outside light came on. Tango leapt into the woods as the crooks raced out the door with ropes. Koko was expecting them and bolted for the woods. Stewart tried to loop a rope around Koko, but the little dog dodged it and disappeared into the dark woods. While Willard guarded Moochee, Benny and Stewart shined flashlights into the woods.

Glancing toward the cabin, Koko spotted Tango on the roof. Tango hissed at Willard. The big man turned away from Moochee to watch Tango walk along the edge of the roof. Moochee began to chew on the rope.

Koko ran out of the woods and headed toward the lake. Stewart and Benny chased after him.

Tango kept squatting down like he was getting set to pounce on the crook below him. Willard gripped the club in his hands, ready to clobber the cat if he pounced.

Koko continued to weave through the woods. To keep attention focused on him, Koko would race out into the open areas every few minutes. Everything was going according to plan. Moochee bit through the rope and trotted toward the woods. Still watching Tango, Willard didn't notice Moochee was gone. A section of the rope was still around Moochee's neck and trailed a few feet behind him. The rope became tangled in a bush, and Moochee struggled to get free.

From the woods, Koko spotted Moochee tugging on the tangled rope. Benny and Stewart saw Moochee, too, and headed toward him.

Those crooks will get to Moochee before he can get free, Koko reasoned. The little dog ran behind Stewart and nipped him on the leg. Stewart spun around and dove at Koko. He barely grabbed Koko's hind leg, but the little dog pulled free. Dodging a rope thrown by Benny, Koko ran hard toward the lake.

As he turned to check on Moochee, Willard finally noticed the dog was gone. Tango jumped to the ground, faked a leg injury, and slowly limped away. When Willard heard the cat hit the ground, he spun around toward Tango. But Koko also thought Tango was hurt. As Willard raised his club and charged toward the cat, Koko ran to help his new friend.

Stewart and Benny were behind Koko and on either side of him. Willard was in front of Koko with his back to the dog, focusing his attention on Tango. Meanwhile, Moochee had pulled loose from the rope. Koko spotted him run out of the woods and into the cabin. Suddenly, Tango broke into a fast run and sprang over a bush into the woods.

When the little dog saw Willard stop and turn toward him, he put on the brakes. As Koko spun around, he realized he was in the middle of the three crooks. The thieves began to slowly advance toward the little dog.

Tango ran out of the woods and sprang onto Willard's back. The big man tried to grab him with his hand, but Tango jumped to the ground. Benny and Stewart threw ropes at Koko, but he was already running toward Willard. Stewart's rope looped around Koko's tail. As the rope began to tighten, Koko sped forward and his tail slipped out of the rope. As Koko ran past Willard's leg, he felt Benny's rope brush his side.

"I've got him!" Benny yelled, as he jerked the rope tight.

"Stop tugging on the rope!" Willard hollered. "You lassoed my foot, you moron."

As Koko led the crooks away from the shack, he saw Tango run into the cabin. Flashlight beams shown all around the area, but the little black dog was hard to see in the dark. Koko crawled through the bushes while glancing toward the cabin. Moochee and Tango were still in there. Koko realized he had taken too long looking at the cabin when a light shown on him. Suddenly, a rope looped over his hind legs! Koko tried to jump free, but the rope held tight. Stewart pulled the little dog over the ground toward him.

Just then, Koko heard a thud in the cabin and saw Tango run out the door. The cat raced toward Koko. Willard and Benny tried to catch the speedy Siamese, but Tango dodged past them. As Stewart grabbed Koko, Tango swiped the crook's hand with his claws. Releasing Koko, Stewart slapped Tango's rear end as the cat jumped away. The blow knocked Tango sideways, but he quickly recovered in time to dodge Willard's club.

Koko began running, but he still had the rope tied to one hind leg and trailing behind him. Stewart stepped on the rope, jerking him to a halt. As Koko tried to back out of the loop, Benny lunged and grabbed him from behind. The little dog twisted back and forth, snapping at Benny's fingers. Stewart bent down and untied one of Willard's shoes.

"What are you doing?" cried Willard.

"I need your shoelace to tie the mutt's mouth shut," Stewart answered.

Stewart tied a little loop in the shoelace. He was trying to place it over Koko's mouth when Willard tapped him on the shoulder.

"What do you want?" growled Stewart.

"It's the other dog!" Willard exclaimed. "He just came out of my cabin carrying the bag of jewels in his teeth."

"What!" Stewart shouted. "Willard, go get that burlap bag out of the van, put a rock in it, and bring it back here. Here, Benny, take this shoelace and tie the little dog's mouth shut; then give the dog to Willard."

Moochee had already disappeared into the woods. Koko continued to snap at Benny's fingers every time he tried to tie the shoelace around his mouth.

As Stewart trotted in the direction that Moochee had taken, he shouted, "Willard, shove the little dog in the burlap bag, tie it shut, and throw the bag into the lake. Benny, hurry up and help me search the woods for that other mutt!"

When Willard returned with the bag, Benny handed Koko to Willard and ran after Stewart. Koko's mouth was tied but not very tightly; he'd already loosened the shoelace some. Willard held the bag in one hand and a struggling little dog in his other. As if that weren't enough, he heard a hissing sound behind him.

Chapter Seven
Drowned in the Lake

Willard turned and spotted Tango behind him. The cat began to circle behind Willard again. Willard kept turning to keep Tango in view.

Things didn't look good for Koko. Moochee was free, but Koko was captured. After several tries, Willard was able to shove the struggling dog into the bag and hold it closed. There was a small hole in the bag through which Koko could see.

Tango continued to circle Willard as the big man kept turning to keep the cat in sight. As he turned, the shoe without a lace came off his foot. Willard tried to put his shoe back on, but he couldn't do it without releasing the bag. He was forced to carry his shoe in one hand and the bag with Koko in the other. Koko began pushing on the shoelace tied around his mouth with his paws.

Things didn't look too good for the crooks, either. Moochee had disappeared into the woods with the jewels. Tango continued to harass Willard. The big man tried to walk backward down the hill toward the lake to keep the cat in sight. Trying to tie a knot in the bag while holding on to his shoe, Willard stumbled downhill.

Inside the burlap bag, Koko continued to push the shoelace from around his mouth. From the shouts coming from the woods, Koko could tell that Stewart and Benny hadn't found Moochee.

Willard stepped on a sharp rock and nearly dropped the bag. Eventually, he reached the short pier at the edge of the lake. By that time, Koko had pushed the shoelace off his mouth. Willard threw his shoe at Tango and missed. The thief had succeeded in tying a loose knot in the bag when he saw Tango squatting on his shoe.

"Don't you dare, cat!" Willard yelled as he charged up the hill. He retrieved his shoe before Tango could use it as a bathroom and hurried toward the pier again.

But Tango was not giving up on Koko. As Willard put his foot on the pier, Tango pounced on his back. Willard tried to hit Tango with his shoe, but hit himself on the back instead. Tango sprang to the ground and ran up the hill. The shoe bounced out of Willard's hand and splashed into the water. As Willard bent down to retrieve his shoe from the shallow water, the knot in the bag loosened a little more. Shuffling backward along the pier while holding on to his wet shoe, Willard kept his eye on Tango.

Maybe I can make the hole in the bag bigger, Koko thought. He bit the inside of the bag, pulled hard with his teeth, and wiggled.

The hole wasn't getting much bigger, but the wiggling made it harder for Willard to hold on to the bag.

Suddenly, Willard got a splinter in his shoeless foot. He began hopping on one foot and lost his balance. As he fell backward, he yelled and threw the bag into the air. His three-hundred-pound body smashed onto the pier, and his big bottom broke through three of the wooden planks. He became wedged in the pier, with his feet in the air and his back end in the water. The bag containing Koko splashed into the water and began to sink.

Inside the bag, Koko could see a small opening at the top. When the bag hit the water, Koko pushed his head out of the opening. The little dog struggled to get free as he sank beneath the water. The bag sank to the bottom of the lake just as Koko pushed out of the bag and swam to the surface.

Willard knew the bag hit the water, but he couldn't see what had happened. Looking like a large turtle on its back, he struggled to get free of the pier. In the dark, he never saw Koko swim to the edge of the lake and hide behind a bush. From his hiding place, the little survivor watched Willard put his shoe down to push up on the dock with both hands. Just as the big man pulled loose from the pier, there was a splash behind him. Tango had dragged his shoe to the edge of the pier and pushed it into the water again.

As Willard waded in the dark water to find his shoe, Koko trotted up the hill to the cabin, and Tango raced up the slope behind him. Willard had left the van's rear door open, and Koko

spotted a small gray bucket in it. (Actually, the bucket was yellow, but dogs can't see all the colors that humans can.) Koko jumped up in the van, grabbed the bucket handle in his teeth, and started to drag it when he heard Willard coming. He jumped to the ground and hid in a clump of bushes. A very wet Willard clomped up the hill and entered the cabin.

"We need to separate and search for Moochee," Koko told Tango.

Tango headed in the direction Stewart and Benny had taken. The first place Koko looked was on top of the hill where they usually met, but Moochee wasn't there. He did see flashlights shining at the bottom of the hill. When Stewart and Benny started up the hill, Koko ran down the other side. The little dog saw a flash of white as Tango ran through the woods. The cat was headed back in the direction of the cabin.

I'll head in the direction Tango went, Koko thought. *But I need to move quietly since Willard is in the cabin.* Koko saw Willard sitting on a chair in the shack. Willard was threading a piece of cord through the shoelace holes in his wet shoe. Just then, Tango came out of the woods on the other side of the dirt road with Moochee. They headed down the road with Moochee dragging the jewel bag in the dirt. Koko ran to meet them.

"Moochee, you look tired," noted Koko. "Do you want me to carry the bag for a while?"

Moochee dropped the bag, and Koko dragged it down the dirt road to the pavement. The dogs and cat went across the paved road and into the woods. In a little while, they stopped and rested in a clump of bushes. Tango climbed a tree and rested between a large branch and the tree trunk.

"We should be safe over here till morning," Moochee reasoned. "The crooks will get tired of searching and go to bed in another hour or so."

The three went to sleep but were awakened by the snap of a stick. Koko and Moochee were instantly awake. A flashlight beam shone on Tango in the tree.

"There's the white cat," whispered Benny. "The dogs and the jewels must be close by."

"*Dog* and the jewels," Stewart corrected him. "Willard drowned the little dog in the lake."

Moochee grabbed the bag of jewels with his teeth and ran away from the bad men. Benny chased after Moochee. Stewart and Willard angled to either side of the fleeing dog. Koko was to the right side of Moochee, between Benny and Willard, but the crooks didn't see him in the dark. Suddenly, Moochee yipped as he ran into a thorn bush. He dropped the bag of jewels to the ground. Before Moochee could retrieve the bag, Benny broke through the bushes next to him. Moochee ran for it, and Benny picked up the bag of jewels.

Chapter Eight
Vanishing Jewel Bag

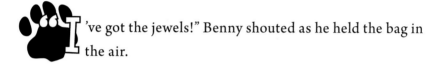I 've got the jewels!" Benny shouted as he held the bag in the air.

Koko ran out of the bushes behind him, bit him on the leg, and dashed back into the brush.

Benny shrieked at the top of his lungs, tossed the bag in the air, and hopped around holding his leg. Koko heard Moochee barking at the top of a hill.

"Tango," Moochee barked, "the bag of jewels is stuck in the tree several feet above the bad man. Try to get the bag before they spot it."

Stewart and Willard ran through the brush to Benny.

"What's wrong?" Willard asked. "Why did you scream like a little baby?"

"A wild animal attacked me from the rear and mauled my leg," Benny whined. "When I turned around, all I could see was a black shape crashing through the brush. It might have been a black panther."

"Wow, a panther," whispered Willard. "You're lucky to be alive."

"There aren't any black panthers in Georgia!" Stewart screamed.

Koko watched from the bushes as Tango crept along a limb above the men and stuck his head through the bag handle. He lifted up his head, and the bag of jewels slid off a branch and onto his back. The jewel bag swung down and Tango clutched the limb with his claws.

Uh oh, Koko thought. *The bag is too heavy for Tango. I hope he doesn't fall. Stewart and his gang are below him.*

Tango stood up on the limb. The bag handle hung around his neck and behind his right front leg.

Benny turned around and showed Willard and Stewart the back of his leg.

"The panther sunk his teeth in my left leg," he whined. "How bad does it look? Do I need to go to a hospital?"

"All I see is a small hole in your leg and a few drops of blood," Willard observed.

"I don't care about your so-called attack!" shouted Stewart. "Where are the jewels?"

Tango had moved near the end of the limb. His weight made the limb bend down till it rested on the limb of another tree. Koko watched as Tango struggled to cross over to the other limb.

"What did you do with the jewels?" Stewart yelled again.

"I threw the bag in the air," Benny answered.

Stewart and Willard shined their flashlights on the ground around them.

"Where did the bag land?" demanded Stewart.

"I never heard it hit the ground," Benny recalled.

Stewart began to shine his flashlight in the tree. As Tango stepped off the limb to the other tree, the limb he was on sprang up, making a rustling noise. Stewart shined his light in the other tree and spotted Tango with the jewel bag.

"Benny, climb that tree and take those jewels away from that cat!" Stewart ordered.

Koko watched Benny go to the tree trunk and try to pull up on a low limb. Tango was about six feet above him with the bag hanging down from his body. Koko could tell its weight pulled heavily on Tango as he slowly moved up the tree.

Benny had his feet and both hands around the limb but couldn't pull himself onto the limb. He just hung there, upside down like a sloth.

"Help Benny," Stewart ordered Willard.

Willard walked under Benny and shoved him up. Benny began to climb after Tango. The cat had moved onto a large limb and tried to cross to another tree. This limb was very thick and didn't bend down from the weight of Tango and the bag. Tango was twenty feet from the ground, and the limb on the other tree was a foot below him. He couldn't move any further toward the end of the limb because of a branch growing up in front of him. Tango was trapped.

Benny reached the limb that Tango was on and slowly moved toward the cat. As Tango tried to go around the branch, he nearly fell. Willard was below him, ready to grab him and the jewels if he did fall.

I need to be ready to help if Tango falls, Koko thought. *I'll move close behind Willard and bite him if it becomes necessary.*

Benny moved to within five feet of Tango. He slowly scooted forward another foot but was still too far away to reach the cat. As Benny moved even closer, the limb began to bend down from his added weight. When he was two feet from Tango, Benny reached for the feline just as the two limbs touched. Tango quickly jumped to the other tree.

Benny lunged at the cat. His finger brushed Tango's tail before he lost his balance and fell from the tree. Willard stood paralyzed as he watched Benny crash through the limbs above him. He made a loud huffing noise when Benny landed on him. As Willard fell backward, Koko had to jump out of the way. The two men tumbled head over heels down a hill.

Koko heard the two crooks moaning and snuck through the bushes to see what had happened to them. He spotted them on their backs at the bottom of the hill.

"You clowns get off your backs and help me get that cat!" shouted Stewart as he picked up a stick to throw at Tango.

Benny was the least hurt, because he had landed on Willard, which was like falling on a fluffy pillow. He slowly walked up the hill while Willard crawled up the hill on his hands and knees. Koko hid in the bushes as Benny walked past and picked up a stick to throw at Tango. Willard was halfway up the hill when Moochee ran up the hill behind him and grabbed his pant's leg in his teeth. Moochee pulled backward, and Willard fell on his face. Willard couldn't see what was dragging him down the hill.

"Help!" yelled Willard. "Either the panther or a wolf has me and is dragging me to his lair."

Moochee dragged him to the bottom of the hill and then ran into the woods.

"Hang on!" shouted Benny, running and waving his stick in the air. "I'm coming to rescue you."

Benny tried to run downhill, tripped, and rolled down the hill into Willard. Again, they lay on the ground, moaning. Stewart stood at the top of the hill, fuming with rage. He was less than five feet from Koko, hiding in the darkness of the bushes. Stewart threw a stick at Benny, who was lying on top of Willard.

"Get up here!" Stewart screamed. "You morons can't do anything but fall out of a tree or down a hill."

While Stewart hollered insults at his gang, Koko backed away. He neared the tree where an exhausted Tango waited. Tango couldn't hold the bag any longer and let it fall to the ground. When the bag hit the ground, Stewart was still busy yelling at his men and didn't turn around. Koko ran to the bag and began to drag it away as fast as he could.

Stewart and the others returned to the tree. Moochee was at the top of the hill and saw Koko take the bag. He began barking to cover any noise Koko made as he dragged the bag away. Benny and Willard threw sticks at Tango, who was forty feet above them. One of the sticks fell down and hit Stewart on the head.

"Stop throwing sticks at the cat!" Stewart bellowed. "The cat is too high for you to hit him, and he doesn't have the bag anymore. Look for the bag on the ground. The cat must have dropped it. One dog is on the hill, and the other is at the bottom of the lake, so the bag must be on the ground."

The crooks searched the area while Tango and Moochee crept away to join Koko. After fifteen minutes of searching, the men quit looking. "Who or what has the jewels now?" Stewart exclaimed.

"Maybe the panther has them," Benny answered.

Stewart picked up a stick and broke it over Benny's head.

Chapter Nine
Trouble in the Gang

Koko, Moochee, and Tango moved further into the woods and went to sleep. The next morning, they were awakened by the sound of a motor running. Koko spotted Benny on the motorbike, driving through the woods. Benny was getting closer to their hiding place.

"Moochee, pick up the jewel bag. We need to leave before we're spotted," Koko whispered.

The dogs weaved their way through the trees, away from Benny. Tango leapt from a tree limb to the ground. The cat hit the ground running. Benny saw him jump from the tree and headed after Tango.

"We'd better see if Tango needs help," Koko barked.

Koko and Moochee ran after Benny. Standing at the edge of a field, they could see the chase. Although Tango was a fast cat and had a good lead on Benny, the motorbike was gaining on the feline. Benny was almost on him when Tango turned sharply to the right. Benny tried to make a sharp right turn, and the motorbike slid out from under him. Tango ran in the opposite direction from where Koko and Moochee were hidden. Moochee set the bag down to rest his mouth.

"Tango is either confused about where we are, or he's leading Benny away from us," said Moochee.

"If I know Tango, he's luring Benny away," Koko concluded. "Let's continue in the woods and see what's ahead of us."

"Okay," sighed Moochee. "But I'm getting tired of carrying this jewel bag."

"I have a plan that will make the bag a lot lighter for you," Koko replied.

"How can you make it lighter?" Moochee asked.

"We can remove the jewels from the bag and put them in another container," Koko explained. "I know how to open the bag. The little metal thing at the top of the bag got caught on a bush, and when I pulled on the bag, it started to open. When I pulled the metal thing the other way, the opening closed." Koko continued, "I saw a bucket in the back of the van. We'll swipe the bucket, open the bag, take out the jewels, and put them in the bucket. We can dig up some grass and put it in the bag to make it look full and then close the bag again."

"You make it sound easy," said Moochee. "But I bet we'll have problems, as usual."

"Think positive, Moochee," Koko barked.

"Okay, I'm positive we'll have problems," Moochee stated. "How do we get the bucket out of the van?"

"We'll think of a way to get it," Koko insisted.

The dogs moved through the woods until they came to a road. Staying in the shadows of the dark woods, Koko looked down the road. He spotted Stewart's van parked several hundred feet away. He could hear voices coming from it.

"Moochee, stay hidden in the woods, and I'll sneak closer to the van," said Koko. "Maybe I can find out what they're up to."

Koko made his way through the woods and drew close to the van. Willard was fussing with Stewart.

"You're telling me you can fence those jewels for one hundred and twenty-five thousand dollars," Willard questioned, "and Benny and I would get twenty-five thousand apiece? Then you would get seventy-five thousand dollars."

"That's right," Stewart declared. "I planned the robbery. I robbed the jewelry store, and I know where to fence the jewels. So, I should get most of the money."

"That's not fair!" Willard shouted. "We should get more money."

"Benny was supposed to cut the power to the alarms. He cut the power to the lights, and the alarms went off when I entered the building!" Stewart angrily replied. "Luckily, the fire department thought the heat of the fire set off the alarms. And all you had to do was drive the getaway van. I came out of the store with the bag of jewels, and there was no van outside."

"Benny and I were hungry and stopped to get a burger," Willard retorted. "We were only a couple of minutes late."

"You're just lucky I wasn't packing a gun!" Stewart yelled. "I'd have shot the both of you!"

Willard reached over and grabbed Stewart by the shirt.

"Well, give me more," Willard threatened, "or there'll be trouble. Twenty-five thousand is enough for Benny, but I want forty. That will still leave sixty for you."

"Sure, that'll be okay," answered Stewart. "Forty for you, sixty for me, and Benny gets twenty-five."

Willard let go of Stewart's shirt. Koko could see an evil look on Stewart's face when the bad man turned away from Willard.

Koko heard the motorbike approaching the van.

"Hi, guys," Benny greeted them. "I chased that orange-and-white cat all over the place. He's probably so tired he wouldn't be able to lift his tail."

"Did you get him?" Willard asked.

"Nope, I lost his trail in the forest," Benny replied.

"Why are you wasting time chasing the cat?" asked Stewart. "The cat doesn't have the jewels. Find the dog! If any animal has the jewels, it would be the dog! Now open up the door at the back of the van and take out the gas can. Fill up the gas tank on the motorbike so it won't run out of gas. Then go and find us something to eat."

"Where can I find food?" Benny asked.

"Either buy it from a store or steal it from a farmhouse," Stewart snapped.

Benny put gas in the motorbike, cranked it up, and drove down the road. Koko returned to where Moochee was resting. He told him about how Stewart and Willard were fighting.

"I have a plan to get that bucket out of the van," barked Koko. "But it will be a little risky."

Just then, Tango walked up to the boys. "What's up, guys?"

"Maybe my plan won't be as risky as I thought," Koko replied.

Tango and Moochee cocked their heads and stared at him.

"If Tango can carry a bag of jewels, he shouldn't have trouble carrying an empty bucket," Koko stated.

Chapter Ten
Ghost Dog

Koko explained his plan to Moochee and Tango.

"The plan still sounds risky," Moochee sighed. "But count me in."

"The plan sounds exciting to me," purred Tango. "The danger makes me tingle all over."

"Now remember, Moochee, if you spot Benny on the motorbike, run off the field and into the woods. Drop the bag of jewels if you have to," Koko cautioned. "Tango, don't go in the van unless both men are chasing Moochee. I'll be in the woods, watching to make sure everything goes as planned and to help anyone in trouble."

"Plans seldom work the way we plan them," added Moochee.

Moochee trotted off toward the field with the bag of jewels. Tango headed in the opposite direction, toward the van. Koko waited in the woods halfway between the field and the van. A nasty puddle full of dead leaves was between him and the road. The little dog figured the puddle would slow down anyone in pursuit that headed his way.

In a few minutes, Koko saw Moochee drag the bag of jewels onto the road. Moochee tugged at the bag like he was too weak to lift it. A few seconds later, Stewart and Willard jumped out of the van and ran toward Moochee. Koko saw his friend drag the bag across the road and into the field. Since the two crooks were focused on Moochee, they didn't see Tango spring from the woods and leap through the open van window. Koko ran to the edge of the woods and watched as Stewart and Willard chased Moochee across the field. Koko looked for Benny, but he was nowhere to be seen.

Good, the plan is working, thought Koko. He looked back at the van and saw a flash of white leap up between the van seats before falling backward. *Uh oh, Tango is having trouble with the bucket.*

Koko turned back to the field and saw Willard headed toward the van. Moochee had the bag in his mouth and was staying ahead of Stewart. *I need to keep Willard from going to the van*, thought Koko. An idea came to him, and he ran to the mud puddle.

It looks really yucky, but I have to do it, he decided. Koko jumped in the puddle and rolled in the nasty water. He hid in the shadows between some bushes, his fur covered with muddy water. As Willard neared Koko's hiding place, the little dog turned his bad eye toward Willard. Koko couldn't see him, but he knew where the crook was from the sound of his footsteps. As Koko watched the van with his good eye, he saw Tango claw his way to the top of the seats with the bucket around his neck. A second later, Tango fell backward again.

"Ahhwoooo," howled Koko.

Willard jumped in the air and stared hard into the woods. Koko knew that Willard would see a wet and muddy little dog with a pale eye staring at him.

"Ahhh!" hollered Willard. "It can't be you. You drowned in the lake. You're dead."

"Ahhwoooo," howled the little dog, as he took a small step forward.

"Go away!" Willard screamed. "I didn't want to drown you. Stewart made me throw you in the lake. Stay away from me!"

Willard turned and fled toward the field again. Koko could hear his feet slapping the pavement as he ran. Koko heard something hit the road behind him and saw the bucket rolling away from the van. Just then, Tango jumped from the back of the van. Koko ran to him and grabbed the bucket handle.

"What happened to you?" Tango exclaimed. "You look like you've been swimming in nasty."

"First, tell me what happened to you while I hide this bucket in the woods," Koko replied.

"Well, I jumped into the van easily enough," answered Tango. "I found the bucket was full of oily rags and had to drag the rags out. Then I stepped through the handle, but the bucket kept slipping off my shoulder. I had to put the handle around my neck. When I tried to jump between the seats, the bucket was too big, and it jerked me backward. Then I tried climbing up the back of the seat with the bucket around my neck. I made it to the top of the seat with the bucket choking the life out of me. But the bucket got caught on the top of the seat. It jerked me backward again, and I landed on the bucket. I was hopping mad and attacked the seat. It was while I was clawing and biting the seat that I noticed the back door of the van wasn't closed all the way. I pushed on the door, and it opened. I dragged the bucket to the door, pushed it out, and jumped out of the van."

"Well done," Koko barked. "Listen, I hear the motorbike."

Koko saw Moochee enter the woods. Willard was still running and waving his arms in the air. Stewart ran toward him, while Benny approached both of them on the motorbike. Benny had something strapped to his back and a bag resting across the handlebars. Stewart and Benny reached Willard at the same time.

"What is wrong with you?" Stewart scowled at Willard.

"It was the ghost of that little dog that I drowned in the lake!" shouted Willard. "Its eyes were pink, it was covered with slime, and it shrieked like a ghost!"

"That's ridiculous," scoffed Benny. "You probably saw the black panther that bit me."

"You're both morons!" yelled Stewart. "There's no ghost or black panther in the woods. It sounds to me like the little black dog is still alive."

"I broke into a farmhouse," Benny announced. "I have a bag full of food and a shotgun."

"Well, the shotgun won't kill a panther unless it's really close to you," Willard replied. "And you can't kill the little dog's ghost with it, either."

Stewart gritted his teeth and ground them together.

Chapter Eleven
The Frame-Up

The three friends spent most of the day hiding from the crooks. Koko was going to have to wait until night to carry out the second part of his plan.

They had lost the men and were resting in the field bordering the woods when Koko heard a motorbike. He peered through some bushes. Stewart was driving the bike. Koko didn't know where the other men were until he heard them headed his way. Actually, what he heard first was Benny. He was singing "I am a Happy Wanderer" in a very loud voice. The words of the song rang through the forest.

> "I love to go a-wandering,
> Along the mountain track,
> And as I go, I love to sing,
> My knapsack on my back."

Then Willard joined in on the chorus.

"Val-deri, Val-dera,

Val-deri,

Val-dera-ha-ha-ha-ha-ha,

Val-deri, Val-dera,

My knapsack . . . "

The song was interrupted by Stewart, racing toward them and shouting, "Shut up! Stop singing, you morons! What was the plan we talked about this afternoon?"

"Uh," answered Benny. "You were going to ride around the field on the motorbike to attract the attention of the dogs. While they were watching you, we would sneak up on them. I would shoot them with the shotgun, and we would recover the jewels."

"How in the world can you sneak up on the dogs when you boneheads are singing at the top of your lungs?" Stewart bellowed.

"Sorry," Benny muttered, "I was enjoying the hike in the woods. I guess I forgot we were sneaking up on the mutts."

Stewart snarled. "I can't trust you blockheads not to break out in song. Now stick to the plan. Keep quiet while you're sneaking."

They were close enough for Koko to see a hurt expression on Benny's and Willard's faces. Stewart cranked up the motorbike and drove away. The crooks crept closer to the dogs' hiding place.

"Follow me," said Tango. "I know a place that will slow down those crooks, and the motorbike can't go there."

Koko picked up the bucket, and Moochee carried the bag of jewels. They followed Tango through the brush until they came to a five-foot-deep ravine. Tango jumped down in the ditch like it was nothing. He turned to look up at the dogs.

"What are you waiting for?" the cat urged the two dogs. "It's an easy jump."

"It's an easy jump for you," Koko replied. "But it's a hard jump for me, and Moochee would be injured jumping that far with his stocky body and short legs."

"Well, you better do something," Tango meowed. "Willard and Benny are only a few hundred feet away and headed in this direction."

"Can you make the jump?" asked Moochee.

"Yes," answered Koko. "I see a small ledge two feet below me. I can jump to that and then to the bottom. Getting out will be a different story."

Moochee nodded to Koko. "I'll meet you later at the place near the cabin."

Grabbing the bag in his teeth, Moochee ran toward the open field. The crooks spotted him, and Benny lifted the shotgun. When he heard the boom of the shotgun, Koko could see Moochee running about four hundred feet ahead of Benny. Moochee continued to run as if the pellets from the shotgun didn't hurt him. Stewart raced across the field on the motorbike. A few seconds later, there was another boom, and then a third shot was fired. Moochee entered a thicket of brush and disappeared from sight.

Koko looked back at Benny and heard him shouting.

"What's with this shotgun?" Benny hollered. "The shotgun shells are loaded with hundreds of pellets, but none of them hit the dog!"

"You must not be familiar with shotguns," observed Willard. "You were firing number nine shotgun shells, which have the most pellets but the smallest size."

"What does that mean?" asked Benny.

"It means that the pellets don't travel much past two hundred yards," answered Willard. "The dog was too far away for the pellets to hurt him. The mutt would have to be within forty or fifty yards to receive any damage."

Benny tried to reload the shotgun but couldn't force the shell into the shotgun.

"What's wrong with these shells?" yelled Benny.

"You're trying to put twelve-gauge shells in a twenty-gauge shotgun," answered Willard. "You should have swiped a box of twenty-gauge shotgun shells."

Benny screamed and threw the shotgun and the shells into the woods as Stewart and the motorbike disappeared into the woods after Moochee.

Koko looked down at Tango and told him what had happened. "Moochee should be fine. Benny used the wrong shells in the gun, so none of them hit Moochee. He was able to get into the woods way before Stewart could follow on the motorbike. But Benny and Willard are coming back this way."

Koko could hear Benny and Willard getting closer and the sound of the motorbike growing fainter in the woods. The little dog dropped the bucket in the ditch, jumped down to the ledge, and leapt to the bottom of the ravine.

"Follow me," Tango meowed. "The ditch gets easier to climb up ahead."

Koko picked up the bucket and trotted after Tango. Before the crooks showed up, the cat and dog had disappeared up the ravine.

Near dusk, Koko and Tango joined Moochee at a spot close to the fishing cabin.

"I'm starving, and my mouth hurts from carrying the bag of jewels," Moochee complained.

"I'm sorry about your mouth; my mouth hurts a little from carrying the bucket," Koko consoled his friend.

"I'll go and catch a chipmunk for you to eat," Tango told Moochee.

"A chipmunk won't help," answered Moochee. "Go catch a rabbit instead."

"Rabbits are too big for me to handle," Tango stated. "How would you like a juicy field mouse?"

"Yuck," Moochee replied.

Tango stuck his tail in the air and marched off.

"I think you insulted him," Koko noted. "Next time, just tell him, 'No, thank you.'"

While Tango was gone, Moochee pulled the metal zipper on the bag and poked his head inside. The dogs picked up the jewels with their mouths and dropped them in the bucket. When the bag was empty, they stuffed leaves and grass into it to make it look full again. Moochee zipped it closed and gave the bag to Koko to carry. Moochee picked up the bucket of jewels, and the two dogs moved toward the cabin. A couple of hours later, Tango returned with muddy paws.

"Why are your paws so muddy?" Koko asked.

"I found a nice mud puddle next to the van," Tango replied. "I muddied my paws. Then, I put paw prints up and down the windshield of Willard's van."

They all had a good laugh about that.

It was late at night, and the men were sleeping. Koko went to the door of the cabin and gently pushed on it with his paws. Nothing happened, so Koko returned to his friends. If the door had opened, Koko would have carried out the second part of the plan. Now, it was up to Tango to do it.

Moochee took a diamond necklace out of the bucket and placed it around Tango's neck. Koko and Moochee dragged the bucket of jewels under the cabin while Tango climbed a tree next to the back window. Koko hid the bucket in the darkest spot he could find. Then he moved out from under the cabin to watch Tango leap from the tree to the windowsill. Tango paused for a moment by the open window as the necklace dangled from around his neck. Then he entered the cabin.

Several minutes passed. Everything was very quiet in the cabin. Suddenly, Tango leapt out the window as shouting erupted from the cabin.

Chapter Twelve
Gang Fight

Koko and Tango joined Moochee under the cabin to look up through a crack in the floorboards and listen.

"Something jumped on my chest!" Willard shouted. "It was probably the little dog's ghost."

"What are you talking about?" Stewart yelled.

A light came on in the cabin. Then everything got quiet again.

"Why are you two idiots staring at me?" Stewart asked.

"Because you have a diamond necklace on your pillow," answered Benny.

"Where did the necklace come from?" asked Willard.

Stewart looked down and picked up the necklace.

"I don't know how this necklace got on my pillow," Stewart replied.

"Where are the jewels?" Willard demanded.

"I don't know where the jewels are," Stewart declared.

"I think you caught the dog and took the jewels from him," Willard accused Stewart. "You kept the necklace with you and hid the rest of the jewels. You were going to keep it all for yourself!"

"That's not true," Stewart insisted. "Someone is trying to frame me."

"We're not buying that story!" yelled Willard. "Take us to where you hid the jewels, now!"

"Yeah," Benny added.

"You're nothing but a dirty thief!" Willard screamed.

"We're all thieves," Benny stated.

"Shut up, Benny!" hollered Willard and Stewart at the same time.

Koko, Moochee, and Tango jumped when they heard someone slam into the cabin wall.

"Tell us where the jewels are, or I'll keep pounding you," Willard exclaimed.

Something heavy hit the door of the cabin, and Stewart tumbled out of the shack and onto the ground. Stewart crawled to his feet and was tackled by Benny. Stewart turned and slugged Benny in the face. Benny released Stewart and held his bleeding nose. Just as Stewart made it to his feet, Willard rushed out the door and shoved him against the van. Stewart bounced off the van and ran toward the woods. Willard ran after him, although he didn't stand a chance of catching him.

While all the fighting was going on outside, Tango jumped through the window, grabbed the necklace, and carried it under the shack.

In a few minutes, Willard returned without Stewart. "Benny, go in the cabin and get the necklace," ordered Willard.

As he entered the cabin, Benny wiped blood off his nose with his sleeve. Willard tried to fix the door that was hanging by one hinge. He was hammering the screws back in the middle hinge with a rock when Benny walked out empty-handed.

"I can't find the necklace," said Benny.

"What do you mean you can't find it?" asked Willard. "I took it from Stewart and put it on the table."

"It wasn't on the table, and I didn't see it on the floor," answered Benny. "Maybe the little dog's ghost took it."

"Empty your pockets," Willard demanded. Benny had some weird things in his pockets but no necklace. Then Willard noticed the van windshield. "Look at my windshield!" he wailed.

"You've got paw prints on the windshield," Benny observed. "That cat must have done it."

Willard stared at him. "Get a cloth and clean the windshield," he told Benny.

While Benny cleaned the windshield, Willard went in the cabin and stayed awhile. He came out, eating an apple, then got in the van. Benny got in the passenger seat, and the men drove away. The cabin door was left open.

"I bet they're looking for Stewart," said Koko.

The little dog looked around for Moochee, but he was gone. Koko looked out from under the cabin and saw Moochee running up the steps and into the cabin. A few seconds later, Moochee came out, dragging the bag of food Benny had swiped from the farmhouse. Koko picked up the bag of leaves and grass and followed Moochee into the woods.

The dogs pulled stuff out of the food bag. They ignored the fruit and the food in cans. They divided half a loaf of bread and a pack of crackers. There was peanut butter in a jar, but the dogs couldn't get into it. They found a few potato chips in a bag and ate them. It wasn't much, but it helped fill their stomachs.

"Why don't we just leave," urged Moochee.

"I'm hoping we can get the crooks to keep chasing us," Koko answered. "The longer they stay here, the better the chance that the police will catch them. As long as Stewart is free, we'll have to be on guard against him. He might even come back and harm my human family."

"Yeah," growled Moochee, "I don't want him harming my family."

"We might as well get some rest," Koko advised. "Willard and Benny will ride around all night looking for Stewart, and Stewart will search the woods all night looking for us and the jewels."

"Where can we sleep safely?" Moochee wondered aloud.

"I'm sleeping in a tree," answered Tango.

"We'd probably be safest sleeping under the cabin," Koko proposed. "Besides, I think we should put some of the jewels back in the bag."

"Why should we do that?" questioned Moochee.

"Maybe we can plant the bag of jewels on Benny or Willard and have all of them fighting amongst themselves."

The dogs went under the cabin and emptied the bag. Koko dragged the bucket over to the bag, and Moochee dropped a mouthful of rings into the bag. Koko dropped the diamond necklace in the bag, too. Then he pushed the bucket into the dark corner again while Moochee zipped the bag closed. Koko and Moochee moved to a dark spot, curled up, and went to sleep. Moochee slept with his head on the bag.

Koko was sleeping soundly when Moochee nudged him awake.

"I hear someone walking behind the shack," Moochee whispered.

Koko saw Stewart's legs at the other end of the cabin. Then Stewart bent down and started to slide under the shack where the crawl space was the highest.

Chapter Thirteen
Sheriff Deputies

Stewart must be trying to hide from Benny and Willard under the shack, Koko reasoned. Although Koko was nearly invisible in the darkest spot under the floor, he knew Stewart would see Moochee once his eyes adjusted to the dark. The dogs held very still. Moochee held the bag handle in his mouth.

Suddenly, Tango ran under the shack a few feet in front of Stewart. The cat hissed and spit at him. Stewart tried to grab him, but Tango stayed just out of reach. Koko and Moochee crept from under the shack without Stewart noticing them.

Once Koko and Moochee were safe outside, Tango raced into the woods and joined the dogs. From their hiding place in the brush, they could see Stewart as well as the front of the cabin.

"Thanks for helping us again," Koko told Tango. "Moochee has some of the jewels in the bag, but I had to leave the bucket with most of the jewelry under the shack. Dragging the bucket across the ground would have made too much noise. It's in a dark corner. I hope Stewart doesn't notice it."

As dawn approached, headlights shone down the dirt road. Willard and Benny drove up in the van. The dogs, cat, and Stewart watched as Benny left the van and entered the shack. Willard opened the back of the van and took out a tire iron. Then he entered the cabin. Koko could see Stewart peering through the floor cracks, watching the other two thieves. Koko heard the two men in the shack arguing.

"This is the last time I'm going to ask you, Benny," Willard warned. "If you've hidden the necklace somewhere, tell me, and all will be forgiven. If I catch you with it later, I'll beat you to a pulp."

"For the last time," Benny insisted, "I don't know where the necklace is. Maybe Stewart grabbed it before you threw him through the door. I'm tired; let's get some sleep. I can barely hold my eyes open."

"We can't go to sleep at the same time," Willard stated. "Stewart might come back and murder us in our sleep. You sleep for two hours while I stand guard. Then you can guard me for two hours while I sleep."

"Why don't you sleep first," Benny declared. "I'll stand guard for you."

"You just told me you could barely hold your eyes open!" Willard exclaimed. "I think you want me to fall asleep so you can run off with the diamond necklace."

"I don't have the necklace," Benny wailed, "and I don't trust you not to hurt me in my sleep."

"Well, I don't trust you either!" Willard shouted.

Koko heard the sound of tires coming up the dirt road. Stewart must have heard it, too, because he crawled to a darker spot. As it pulled up and stopped in front of the cabin, Koko recognized the sheriff's car. A radio squawked as the deputy called in to headquarters.

"This is car 212," reported the deputy. "I'm investigating a fishing cabin with a broken front door. Steve in car 299 is searching the area with me. I might need some backup. Tell Steve to turn on the dirt road we passed earlier. Also, see who owns a white van with tag number THF1313."

Willard and Benny were looking out the front window. A car door slammed closed, and the police officer approached the house. The deputy knocked on the door, and Willard opened it.

"Good morning, officer," Willard greeted him with a smile. "How can I help you?"

"I'm investigating this area," the deputy replied. "There was a break-in at a farmhouse not far from here. We believe an escaped criminal named Stewart might be in the area. Have you seen anyone suspicious around here?"

"No, officer," Willard lied. "I haven't seen anyone around here."

"How about your friend in there?" asked the officer. "Has he seen anyone?"

"No, sir, officer sir," Benny stammered.

Just then, another sheriff's car pulled up. The second deputy stayed in the car. Koko noticed that the back door of the van was open, and that gave him an idea. He picked up the bag containing the rings and trotted toward the van. Neither of the deputies could see Koko. But the crook under the cabin could see him. Stewart stared at Koko as the little dog carried the jewel bag in his teeth.

Koko hopped in the van with the bag and placed it behind the driver's seat. He turned to jump out but a car door slammed and the other deputy walked up behind the van. He stood looking at the cabin.

"Do either of you own this cabin?" the first deputy asked Willard.

"It's my cabin," Willard answered.

"How did the door get broken?" the deputy questioned.

"Someone must have broken in while I was gone," Willard responded. "There's nothing to steal except a little food."

"Well, the wood splitters on the ground suggest that somebody or something broke *out* of the cabin," the officer stated.

Willard and Benny didn't say anything for a minute. Finally, Willard suggested, "Maybe the thief got mad when he was in the cabin because there was nothing good to steal and broke the door."

"Well, if he broke the door getting out," stated the police officer, "then how did he get in the cabin?"

Willard and Benny just stood there in silence.

Koko tried to sneak out of the van, but he couldn't jump down without the officer hearing him. He was afraid that the deputy might lock him in his car and take him to the animal shelter.

"Do you mind if I come in and look around?" asked the officer.

"No, not at all," Willard offered.

"Steve, why don't you search the van," suggested the deputy as he entered the cabin.

Chapter Fourteen
Two Down and One to Go

Moochee emerged from the bushes wagging his tail. He ran up to the second policeman. As Moochee put his paws on the officer's pants, the deputy bent down and petted him.

"Sorry, pooch," said the officer, "I've got work to do."

Koko jumped out of the van while the deputy took Moochee's paws off his leg. As the man turned around, he saw Koko behind him, wagging his tail.

"Shoo, dogs; I have work to do."

Moochee moved closer to the fishing cabin. Benny spotted Moochee and pointed.

"Willard, look!" shouted Benny. "It's the chunky dog that swiped our . . ."

Before Benny could finish, Willard slapped a hand across Benny's mouth.

"Benny was going to say, 'the dog that swiped our sandwiches,'" added Willard.

"Is that why you slapped a hand across his mouth?" The first policeman frowned.

"He's always blurting out things like that," answered Willard. "I was just tired of hearing him."

The second police officer began searching the van. Koko trotted over to Moochee and sat down.

"Willard, look!" shouted Benny. "It's the little black dog that Stewart tried . . ."

Willard slapped his hand over Benny's mouth again.

"Did you say *Stewart*?" asked the officer in the cabin.

Neither crook answered the policeman, but they both looked scared. The officer in the van turned to stare at Benny.

The policeman in the shack rubbed his chin for a few seconds and stared at the two crooks. Then he said, "Steve, call in some more backup. Then go back to searching that van. You two, step outside while I check the cabin."

While Steve called for more backup, Koko and Moochee slipped back into the woods. Benny and Willard watched them disappear into the woods but were helpless to do anything about it. Stewart could see them, too. Koko saw Stewart scoot out from under the back of the cabin. Suddenly, he stopped and crawled back under the shack.

The second deputy went back to searching the van while the other officer searched the cabin. Benny and Willard took a step backward toward the woods. They stopped, then took another step closer to the woods. As they started to step back again, Moochee barked.

"The two of you come over here and stand behind the van, where I can keep a better eye on you," ordered Officer Steve.

Willard and Benny glared at the woods where Moochee was hidden and moved behind the van. Another sheriff car pulled up to the cabin. Koko watched Willard and Benny turn pale when they saw the police officer pick up the jewel bag in the van. Then the little dog turned and spotted Stewart dragging the bucket of jewels from under the cabin. The third deputy stepped out of his car.

"Matt," said the officer in the van. "Make sure these two don't go anywhere. Some of the stolen jewels are in this bag."

The third officer drew his gun and pointed it at Willard and Benny.

Officer Steve emerged from the van and walked over to the cabin. He stuck his head in the door.

"Hal," he called to the deputy in the cabin. "Some of the stolen jewels were in the van. You continue searching the cabin. I'm calling in more officers to search the area for Stewart."

"Stewart must have planted the jewels there!" shouted Benny.

Willard started to slap his hand across Benny's mouth again, then shrugged.

"Stewart wouldn't leave any of the jewels," added Willard. "The dogs did it. They must have had the jewels all the time."

"If you're working on an insanity plea," said a policeman, "save it for the judge."

Koko and Moochee moved toward the rear of the cabin. Koko spotted Stewart near the lake, stuffing his pockets with the jewels from the bucket.

"Stewart has the jewels," barked Moochee, "and he's getting away!"

"We can't let that happen," Koko replied. "Stewart is the biggest crook of them all and the most dangerous."

Stewart ran through the woods. Every now and then he'd stop, listen, and look around. Unknown to him, Koko and Moochee followed Stewart for about a mile. Finally, he spotted the dogs. Stewart threw several rocks at them, but the dogs were able to dodge them.

Koko hadn't seen Tango since the police arrived at the fishing cabin. He looked around but didn't see him anywhere. A police helicopter flew close to them, but it was too far away to spot Stewart. While the dogs watched the helicopter, Stewart slipped away.

"Where did Stewart go?" asked Moochee.

"I don't know," Koko answered. "We'll need to move carefully and rely on our ears and noses to find him. He may try to ambush us, so stay alert."

The dogs crept through the woods. Their ears were up, and their noses sniffed the air.

"I smell someone," whispered Koko.

"I hear someone behind that tree," added Moochee.

Just then, Stewart jumped out from behind the tree with a big stick. Koko and Moochee were ready for a surprise attack and bolted for cover. Stewart threw the stick and hit Moochee on his right hind leg. Moochee yipped but kept on running.

"That was close," barked Koko. "Are you okay, Moochee?"

"My leg hurts a little where the stick hit me, but I'm okay."

By noon, Stewart was several miles from the fishing shack. As he reached the end of the woods, he stopped. Ahead of him was a large, open field. Several hundred yards behind that was a large cornfield. Koko reasoned that Stewart was waiting for night before crossing the open area. But night was eight hours away. The dogs sat in the woods and watched Stewart snoozing against a tree.

"I'm hungry," Moochee moaned. "We didn't find enough food to eat, and I feel weak."

"I'm feeling weak and tired, too," Koko replied.

"I'm going to nap while Stewart's sleeping," Moochee barked.

"You go ahead," Koko said. "I'll keep my eye on Stewart. One of us needs to stay awake when he's this close."

Chapter Fifteen
The Cornfield

oochee was sound asleep and snoring. Koko fought to keep his good eye open. The sun was straight up, and the heat made him sleepy. Stewart sat with his back to a tree less than two hundred feet away. His eyes were closed, but Koko wasn't sure he was asleep. Moochee had been sleeping for over two hours.

"Wake up," Koko nudged Moochee. "It's time for me to get some sleep."

Moochee stretched, yawned very wide, and stood up. Koko lay down and closed his eye. He wasn't sure how long he'd been sleeping when something woke him. A faint sound came from the woods behind them. Koko looked over at Moochee, who had fallen asleep again. When he turned in Stewart's direction, he saw that the crook was on his feet and looking all around.

Koko raised his head and sniffed the wind. There was a faint smell of humans. He trotted to the top of a small hill. In the distance, he could make out several policemen searching through the woods and headed his way. Koko looked back at Moochee and saw he was still sleeping.

Stewart must have heard the policemen, too, because he bolted out of the woods and ran into the field. He was running hard toward the distant cornfield.

"Moochee, wake up," barked Koko. "Stewart is on the run, and we need to keep up with him."

Koko's barking alerted the policemen, and they slowly headed in the dogs' direction. Koko and Moochee ran down to where Stewart had been hiding in the woods. Looking back at the hill where they had been standing, Koko saw that the police weren't there yet. By the time the officers reached the top of the hill, Stewart was nearly to the cornfield. Koko and Moochee barked and ran to the edge of the field, but the police weren't looking in their direction. Stewart disappeared into the corn.

"Come on, Moochee," Koko barked. "Let's head for the cornfield and see if the police follow us."

The dogs ran across the first field to the edge of the field of corn, but the police were still looking in the woods. The cornfield was a large one that covered dozens of acres. They didn't see any sign of Stewart.

"Moochee, you stand out here and bark," Koko suggested. "Hopefully, it will attract attention to the cornfield. I'll sneak through the corn and try to find Stewart."

Koko entered the rows of corn very cautiously. His little heart was beating so hard that it pounded in his ears. He sniffed and followed Stewart's scent. Although the crook's scent was very weak, even the faint smell of Stewart made Koko tremble with fear. Koko wasn't as afraid when Moochee and Tango were with him. The little dog listened with his ears cocked up. The only sounds he heard were birds flapping and the wind gently rustling the cornstalks. As he slowly walked between long rows of corn, he sniffed and listened. Stewart's scent seemed to be getting stronger. Koko heard footsteps running to his left and spun around.

Suddenly, Stewart crashed through the cornstalks a few yards from Koko! The little dog ran to his right as fast as he could. He began weaving between the stalks with Stewart close behind. The weaving slowed Koko down, so he turned and ran straight between the rows. Stewart fell farther behind him. Several hundred feet ahead of Koko, the cornfield ended. The little dog raced out of the cornstalks, then put on the brakes.

A large dog stood in front of him. The big dog's head was lowered, his teeth were bared, and a deep growl came from his throat. Moochee's barking had attracted the wrong kind of attention. Koko heard Stewart stop several yards behind him. Koko was trapped between Stewart and a big Rottweiler. The dog slowly moved one step closer to Koko.

I'm the closest one to the Rottweiler, Koko thought. *The big dog will attack me first, so I need to make a run for the cornfield. If I run*

*to the right, I'll be running toward Stewart, and the dog might go
after him. But there's the chance Stewart might kick me toward the
Rottweiler. Then I'd be a goner for sure.*

The little dog turned to his left and ran back into the corn.
Stewart turned right and ran back into the corn as well. The
Rottweiler hesitated for a few seconds, trying to decide which one
to chase. Then he charged after Koko. The little dog ran as hard
as he could between the rows until he heard the big dog crashing
through the cornstalks.

*If I keep running straight ahead, the big dog is going to catch
me. I need to weave between the stalks. My small size will benefit me,
while the Rottweiler's size will slow him down.*

Koko heard the bigger dog crashing into the stalks as he tried
to catch Koko. The Rottweiler tripped over a stalk and crashed to
the ground. Koko took the opportunity to change direction and
run to the right, in the direction Stewart had gone.

I need to catch up with Stewart and pass him, Koko decided.
Then the big dog will attack him instead of me.

Koko ran, but he couldn't pick up Stewart's scent. The crook
was gone, and the big dog was still after him.

Chapter Sixteen
An Old Friend

n the distance, Koko heard Moochee bark that more officers had arrived with a police dog. Koko continued to run in and out of the cornfield looking for Stewart. After colliding with dozens of cornstalks, the Rottweiler had slowed down his chase. Koko spotted Stewart running toward a barn nearly a quarter of a mile away.

Dashing out of the cornfield, the little dog raced toward the barn. The Rottweiler barked, and Koko stopped and turned for a moment. The little dog had more than a hundred-foot lead on the Rottweiler, but he was tiring fast. The big dog was gaining on him. He knew he wouldn't make it to the barn before the Rottweiler caught him. All Koko could do was run hard and hope something would slow the big dog down enough for him to make it to the barn.

A hundred yards ahead of him, Koko glimpsed something white running swiftly toward him. A few seconds later, he recognized Tango. The cat was headed straight toward him and the Rottweiler. When Tango was a few yards away, he leapt in the air and sailed over Koko. The Rottweiler was only a few yards from Koko when the big dog turned and chased after Tango. The cat gave a meow of delight and raced for the cornfield.

I'll never understand cats, thought Koko. *Being chased by a dog eight times his size is fun to him.*

Koko stopped to watch Tango disappear between the cornstalks. A few seconds later, the Rottweiler crashed into the cornfield.

I hope Tango is going to be all right. There aren't any trees close by for him to climb. I need to catch my breath before I get to the barn.

Koko trotted up to the barn. He lay down in front of the barn door. It gave him time to get his breathing back to normal and to think. *Stewart may be waiting just behind the barn door, ready to grab me,* Koko worried. *I'd better be very careful in there. Maybe I should just wait out here and follow him if he leaves the barn. But he could be sneaking out the other side right now. I'm not sure what I should do.*

Koko turned around and spotted the Rottweiler on the edge of the cornfield, looking around. He decided to enter the barn. Getting to his feet, Koko slowly walked toward the barn. When he got close to the open door, Koko dashed through in case Stewart was behind the door. Koko spun around. He didn't see Stewart anywhere, but he could smell him. His muscles tense, Koko was ready to run at the slightest movement.

Stewart's scent was strongest near a big pile of hay. Koko sniffed the air and moved slowly toward the pile. When he was a few feet from the hay, he stopped and listened. Not hearing anything, he moved a little closer. Suddenly, an arm shot out from the hay, and a hand grabbed Koko's front paw!

"Ah ha!" shouted Stewart. "I finally got my hands on you, mutt."

Koko bit his fingers, but Stewart didn't let go of his paw. The evil man stood up and dangled Koko in the air by one foot. That hurt Koko, but he didn't yip. He growled and bared his teeth.

Stewart searched for something in his pocket. Diamond, ruby, and sapphire rings spilled out of his pocket onto the ground. Half the jewels in his right pocket had fallen before he pulled out his hand. Stewart held a pocketknife. He tried to open the knife blade with one hand but couldn't. Stewart put the knife to his mouth and pulled on the back of the blade with his teeth. Koko wiggled and twisted, making it harder for Stewart to hold him with one hand. As Stewart pulled the blade open with his teeth, he lost his grip on Koko. The bad man ran to block the door so Koko couldn't run outside. Keeping his body between Koko and the door, Stewart slowly backed the little dog toward the rear of the barn.

All of a sudden, something large bolted through the door opening! It hit Stewart from behind and knocked him to the ground. A big German shepherd jumped off the crook's back and grabbed the hand holding the knife in its teeth. The big dog

wore a harness that identified him as a police dog. The shepherd dragged Stewart by the hand until the crook dropped the knife. The large dog stood over the crook, growling. Then Koko got a good look at the German shepherd. It was an old friend—Lobo!

A couple of years ago, Lobo, Koko, and Moochee were all stray dogs. Lobo and Moochee had gotten into a fight over food. Koko jumped in to help Moochee, and Lobo attacked him. The German shepherd mauled Koko and blinded the little dog's left eye. Later, Koko found Lobo in bad condition after the shepherd had survived a fight with a pack of coyotes. Lobo had been too weak to feed himself. Taking pity on his old enemy, Koko brought him food and nursed him back to health. After that, they became friends. Koko and Moochee were picked up, taken to a shelter, and adopted. Later, Lobo caught a convict trying to escape from a work detail and became a police dog.

Lobo kept Stewart on the ground until two police officers entered the barn with drawn pistols. The policemen praised Lobo and handcuffed Stewart. One policeman removed the stolen jewels from Stewart's pockets. As one officer took Stewart out of the barn, the other one gathered up the jewels on the ground.

"I was hoping the bad man would try to get away," growled Lobo. "He had a familiar smell I didn't like, and I was ready to give him a good bite."

"He was the convict you caught in the park trying to escape a work gang before you became a police dog," Koko barked. "I'm glad you got here when you did. In a few more seconds, I might have been killed."

"Friends help friends when they're in trouble," Lobo stated. "Besides, it's my job to capture the bad guys."

"It's good to see you again. I'd better go find Moochee. Thanks again," Koko called out as he trotted past the police officer. He stuck his head out of the barn door and spotted Moochee and Tango in a wooded area. He ran happily toward his friends.

More police showed up, and a police helicopter landed in the field. Fifteen minutes later, news helicopters were on the scene. Koko, Moochee, and Tango sat and watched everything from the woods. Koko couldn't help but notice the Rottweiler running in and out of the cornfield. The big dog still hadn't realized that Tango had left the field.

Chapter Seventeen
The Animal Shelter

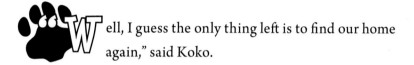 ell, I guess the only thing left is to find our home again," said Koko.

"No," answered Moochee. "We need to find some food and then home."

"What are you going to do?" Koko asked Tango.

"Oh, I'll hang around with you guys for a while," he purred.

They found a road and began to walk in the direction Moochee thought was home. After a while, Moochee spotted an animal shelter.

"Koko, let's go turn ourselves in at the animal shelter," Moochee suggested. "The shelter will give us food to eat."

"That's a good idea, Moochee," Koko agreed. "Our human family will probably check the shelter, looking for us. They may have left a description of what we look like at the shelter. We might be home before it gets dark."

"This is where we part company," Tango added. "A shelter is not for me. It's been fun hanging around you guys. Try not to get in any more trouble without me."

Tango sprinted away and disappeared into some tall grass. Koko and Moochee yelled their thanks for all his help.

"I'm going to miss having Tango around," sighed Koko.

"You'd better keep that kind of talk down," Moochee warned him. "You don't want the other dogs in the shelter to hear that."

Koko and Moochee walked up to the front door of the shelter and scratched on the door. There was a teenage girl in a brown uniform at a desk. She didn't see or hear the dogs, because her back was to the door and she had earphones on her head. Koko could hear the music from the earphones.

"We need to make more noise," barked Moochee.

The two dogs began to bark and scratch on the door. The teenager turned around and yelled at the dogs.

"Go away!" she hollered. "I can't hear my music with all that barking."

Her yelling got the attention of the man in charge of the shelter. He walked in and told her to turn off the headphones and put away her iPod. Then he noticed the dogs at the front door and opened it for them.

"Marsha, there are two strays here that need to be put in a cage and fed. Put them in the isolation cage across from the small dogs in cage four. I've fed and watered the dogs in all the other cages," the man instructed the girl. "I have a lot of things to do without doing your job, too. Now, if you want to keep your summer job, take care of these dogs."

The man watched as the girl led Koko and Moochee to their cage. Four other dogs were in the cage across from them. After she put the two new dogs in the cage, she sat down again. The man hollered for her to put food and water in the containers for the dogs. The teenager poured some water in a long trough and food in another. Moochee was the first one at the food, with Koko right behind him.

"Marsha, I'm leaving for a couple of hours, so you're in charge. Doug from animal control will be by this morning to pick up the two maimed dogs. He's taking them to a shelter that has more traffic to increase their chances of being adopted."

Koko studied the dogs in the cage across from him. He noticed that one dog was missing a leg and another dog had half the fur burned off his back. *I wonder if those are the two dogs the man was talking about,* Koko thought. *I hope they find good homes. I hope Mama and Dad come for us soon, too.*

The man left, and a few minutes later the teenager put the headphones back on and picked up her iPod.

When he finished eating, Koko lay down on the concrete floor next to Moochee. Koko had hoped the shelter would call his human family when he walked in the shelter, but they hadn't. Koko began to worry he might not see his family again.

A little while later, another man came in and said something to the teenager. She pointed to the cage across from Koko and Moochee. The man opened the cage and took away the three-legged dog and the dog with the burn scar on its back. As he passed by, he stopped a moment and stared at Koko.

"Hey!" he yelled at the girl. "Turn the music off."

The teenager turned off the music and took off the headphones.

"I noticed there was a small black dog that only has one eye," said the man. He has little chance of being adopted here. Why don't I take him, too?"

The man pointed at Koko. The girl looked at Koko with his eye missing and his hair matted down from living in the woods.

"Yeah, he doesn't look like much," she answered. "I guess it'll be all right to take him, too."

The girl put on the headphones and picked up her iPod. Koko backed to the rear of the cage. When the man reached for Koko, the little dog growled and bared his teeth. Then Moochee jumped up and growled too. When the man took a step closer, the dogs in the cage across from Koko and Moochee began to growl and bark as well. The man stepped back. The teenager took off her headphones and stared at the dogs with her mouth open.

"What did you do?" she asked.

"I didn't do anything to the dogs," the man insisted. "When I tried to get the little dog, all the dogs turned vicious."

Koko heard the front door open and someone entering the building.

"What's going on?" asked the man who was in charge of the shelter.

"I told this man he could take the little one-eyed dog, but the other dog wouldn't let him," answered the girl. "I thought you would be gone for a couple of hours."

"I was several miles down the road when I remembered a man and woman came in here a couple of days ago looking for a little one-eyed dog. They also described that other dog with him as missing. And for your information, no dogs are to be taken from this facility unless I tell you."

"I . . . I'm sorry," stammered the girl. "I won't let you down again."

The young girl put away her iPod and headphones. The man in charge made a call. Fifteen minutes later, Mama and Dad were there to pick up Koko and Moochee.

The man in charge smiled and said, "I wish all our animals had such short stays with us. It's the strangest thing—they came to our door and barked to be let in. Since they turned themselves in, there won't be a charge for picking them up."

Mama and Dad made a contribution to the shelter anyway to help with the other animals there.

It wasn't long before the dogs were home again. Mama and Dad gave the boys baths and some of their own food. Then they gave them some special treats and lots and lots of hugs. Koko and Moochee curled up on their own beds and had a good night's sleep.

About a week later, Moochee was visiting again. The two friends were resting in the den when Koko heard Mama talking in the kitchen.

"I hope he gets along with the dogs," she told Dad. "He seems like a good cat."

The door opened, and in walked Tango.

"You have a houseguest," meowed Tango.

"How did you find my home?" Koko asked.

"Oh, I have my ways," the feline replied. "I asked all the cats I came across about you and finally picked up your scent. I like it here. The lady gave me some food and a saucer of milk."

"You better not have eaten any of my food," barked Moochee.

"Relax, big guy," Tango purred. "It was cat food, and the man left to buy me a bed. It looks like you have a roommate, Koko. I'm going to like hanging around you two guys."

"Well, life should be even more interesting with Tango around," Koko sighed. "Welcome home, Tango!"

THE END